Karen's Accident

Sara Crawford

**Other books by
Ann M. Martin**

Leo the Magnificat
Rachel Parker, Kindergarten Show-off
Eleven Kids, One Summer
Ma and Pa Dracula
Yours Turly, Shirley
Ten Kids, No Pets
Slam Book
Just a Summer Romance
Missing Since Monday
With You and Without You
Me and Katie (the Pest)
Stage Fright
Inside Out
Bummer Summer

THE KIDS IN MS. COLMAN'S CLASS series
BABY-SITTERS LITTLE SISTER series
THE BABY-SITTERS CLUB mysteries
THE BABY-SITTERS CLUB series

Little Sister

Karen's Accident
Ann M. Martin

Illustrations by Susan Tang

A
LITTLE APPLE
PAPERBACK

SCHOLASTIC INC.
New York Toronto London Auckland Sydney

No part of this publication may be reproduced in whole or in part, or stored in a retrieval system, or transmitted in any form or by any means, electronic, mechanical, photocopying, recording, or otherwise, without written permission of the publisher. For information regarding permission, write to Scholastic Inc., 555 Broadway, New York, NY 10012.

ISBN 0-590-69189-9

12 11 10 9 8 7 6 5 4 3   7 8 9/9 0 1 2/0

Printed in the U.S.A   40

First Scholastic printing, January 1997

The author gratefully acknowledges
Jan Carr
for her help
with this book.

Karen's Accident

Winter Fun

Splat!

Nancy threw a snowball at me. It hit my mitten.

"Hey!" I cried. I picked up a handful of snow and packed it down. "Nancy!" I called. "Watch this!"

Bull's-eye! My snowball hit the middle of her coat.

"Yesss!" I cried.

I love playing outside. I can shout as loudly as I want. Nobody tells me to use my indoor voice.

Mommy pulled back the curtains at the window. She smiled at us.

"Hi, Mommy!" I waved to her.

Maybe you are wondering who I am. My name is Karen Brewer. I live in Stoneybrook, Connecticut. I am seven years old and in the second grade. When I am all bundled up to play in the snow, you cannot see my hair. But it is blonde. My eyes are blue and I have freckles. I also have glasses. They get fogged up in the cold.

Nancy Dawes is one of my best friends. I am lucky. I have two best friends. The other is Hannie Papadakis. Nancy lives next door to me at the little house. (I will tell you all about the little house soon.)

"Come on," I called to her. "Let's go up in the tree house. We can have a secret snowball meeting."

Nancy and I climbed up the ladder and sat in the tree house. We looked down at all the white, white snow.

"What is a *secret* snowball meeting?" she asked.

2

"It is when we think of all the things we did over winter vacation," I said. "The things we loved the best."

Nancy took a moment to think.

"I will start," I said. "I liked going sledding."

"I liked building snowpeople," said Nancy. "And I liked getting presents for Hanukkah."

"I liked watching Irina Kozlova on TV," I said. Irina Kozlova is a figure skater. She is from Russia. When she skates, she looks like a beautiful ballerina. "Irina Kozlova is my favorite," I added.

"She is my favorite too," agreed Nancy.

"I wish I had her feather costume," I said. I pictured myself dressed like Irina. "I would look very good in a costume like that."

Just then Andrew came outside. Andrew is my little brother. He is only four. He was carrying my magic wand. Andrew likes to play with my things.

"Can I come up?" he asked.

"It is a *secret* snowball meeting," I shouted down.

Nancy whispered in my ear. "He could wave the wand and say some magic words. That would be a good thing to do at a secret meeting."

"Okay," I told him. "You can come up. But you have to do everything we say."

Andrew climbed up the steps.

"Here," I said. I reached down to help him. "Hand the wand to me."

Andrew was not very good at saying magic words for our secret meeting. He shouted "Kaboom!" He wanted to pretend he was a superhero. But we did not get to play for very long. Mommy called us inside. She made us cocoa.

"Are you ready to go back to school tomorrow?" she asked.

School! Yikes! I had almost forgotten about school.

Andrew licked his cocoa mustache. "Do we go to the big house then?" he asked.

5

"No," said Mommy. "It is only January. You will go to the big house in February."

"In February when it is Easter?" asked Andrew.

"No," I told him. "In February when it is *Valentine's Day*."

Sometimes Andrew gets confused. He is little. But that is not the only reason. It is easy to get confused when you are a two-two.

A Very Busy Two-Two

What is a two-two? Two-two is a name I made up for Andrew and me. (I thought of it after I heard a story called *Jacob Two-Two Meets the Hooded Fang*.) I call us that because we have two of lots of things. You see, Andrew and I do not always live with Mommy. We have two houses. And two families. And two sets of clothes to wear, one at each house. Let me explain.

When I was little, Andrew and I lived with Mommy and Daddy. We all lived in a big house. It was the house that Daddy

7

grew up in. But Mommy and Daddy started to fight a lot. They decided that they did not love each other anymore. They still loved Andrew and me very much. But they wanted to get a divorce.

So Mommy and Andrew and I moved to the little house. After a while, Mommy married another man. He is a carpenter and his name is Seth. Now he is my stepfather. Seth has a dog named Midgie and a cat named Rocky. They live with us too. And so does my pet rat, Emily Junior, and Andrew's hermit crab, Bob.

But Andrew and I do not live with Mommy and Seth all the time. We live there every other month. The rest of the time we live at the big house with Daddy.

Let me tell you about the big house. It is a good thing it is big. *Sooooo* many people live there. Daddy got married again to a woman named Elizabeth. She is my stepmother. She already had four children, so now I have three stepbrothers and a stepsister. Sam and Charlie are in high school.

Kristy is thirteen. (She is the greatest baby-sitter ever.) And David Michael is seven, like me. (He can be a pain sometimes. But he and I go to different schools. I go to Stoneybrook Academy.)

But that is not all! Daddy and Elizabeth adopted a little girl from a faraway country called Vietnam. Her name is Emily Michelle. (I love her so much that I named my rat after her.) Emily Michelle is two and a half. When she came to live with us, Nannie came too. Nannie is Elizabeth's mother, so she is my step-grandmother. She helps take care of Emily Michelle. Actually, she helps take care of all of us.

Do you think that is enough people for one house? You can see why Andrew gets confused.

Now I will tell you about the big-house pets. There is Shannon. She belongs to David Michael. She is a big Bernese moun-tain dog puppy. Then there is Boo-Boo. He is Daddy's grouchy old cat. And Andrew and I have big-house pets too. We have Crystal Light the Second and Goldfishie. Guess what they are. I will give you a hint. They are gold and they live in a fish tank.

At first it was not easy to live in two houses. I kept forgetting things. Like Tickly, the special blanket that I sleep with. But I had a good idea about Tickly. I tore it into two pieces. Now I do not have to pack up Tickly every time I move from one house to another. I also have two stuffed cats, Moosie and Goosie. I keep one at each house.

Remember I told you I have two best friends? Nancy lives next to my little house. Hannie lives across the street from my big house. Isn't that perfect?

Phew! It is pretty busy being a two-two. Lucky for me, I am *very* good at being busy. And lucky for Andrew, I am his big sister. I can always help him when he gets confused.

"Is tomorrow still vacation?" he asked.

"No," I said. I took a last sip of cocoa. "Tomorrow we go back to school."

Back to School

"Hello, everybody," Ms. Colman said. Ms. Colman is my teacher. She is the most *gigundoly* wonderful teacher in the whole world. "Did you all have a nice vacation?"

I was standing in the back of the classroom with Hannie and Nancy. I hurried to my seat. I shot up my hand.

"I had a *wonderful* vacation," I told her. "I went sledding. And I made snowpeople. And Mommy made us cocoa. And Andrew thought Easter was in February, and — "

"It sounds as if you were busy, Karen." Ms. Colman laughed.

"*Very* busy." I nodded.

Ms. Colman looked around the room. "I am glad to see you all again," she said. "Ricky, would you take attendance?"

Ricky Torres sits next to me, in the front of the classroom. He wears glasses, like I do. All the glasses wearers sit up front. (Not only that, Ricky is my pretend husband. We got married one day on the playground.)

I nudged Ricky's arm. "I am here," I whispered, in case he did not see me.

Ricky got the attendance book and looked around the room. Nancy and Hannie were there, of course. And Natalie Springer was there. She can be shy, but she is nice. Bobby Gianelli waved hello to me from across the room. He used to be a bully, but now he is (usually) my friend. Pamela Harding was there. (I call her my best enemy.) And Addie Sidney. And Terri and Tammy Barkin, the twins. . . .

"Thank you, Ricky," said Ms. Colman.

Ricky had finished taking attendance. Everyone was present.

"It is good that everyone is here," said Ms. Colman. "Because I have some very special projects planned."

I sat up taller in my seat. Ms. Colman thinks of *very* good projects.

Ms. Colman went to the blackboard. "What I would like you all to do," she said, "is think of some people you admire."

Sara Ford raised her hand.

"Harriet Tubman," she said.

I knew about Harriet Tubman. She was a slave who escaped to freedom and then helped other slaves escape. Ms. Colman had taught us about her when we were studying history.

"That is a very good choice," said Ms. Colman. "But I want you to think of someone who is alive. We are going to write letters to the people on our list. We will tell them why we admire them."

Ooh, this was going to be fun.

"Can you each think of someone you ad-

13

mire?" Ms. Colman picked up a piece of chalk.

I did not have to think long. I turned around and mouthed my answer to Nancy. (I was trying very hard not to shout out.)

"What was that, Karen?" Ms. Colman asked.

"Irina Kozlova," I said aloud.

"She is a beautiful skater," said Ms. Colman. "Is that why you admire her?"

"I admire her because she looks like a ballerina," I said. "And she has beautiful costumes."

Ms. Colman wrote *Irina Kozlova* on the board.

Other kids in the class began getting ideas too. Hannie wanted to write to the First Lady. And Bobby wanted to write to Stan "The Man" Jackson. (I think he is a basketball player.) But I hardly paid attention. I was already thinking of the letter I would write.

"Dear Irina Kozlova," I would say. "You are a very beautiful skater. I especially love

14

your costumes. I wish I could have a costume like yours. Where can I get one? Do you buy yours at a special store?"

I got out my pencil and paper. I started to write the letter.

"And what do you think about Addie's idea, Karen?" asked Ms. Colman.

Uh-oh. I had been busy writing. I had not been paying attention.

"Hmm?" I asked. I did not have any idea what Addie had said. "I was writing my letter," I tried to explain.

"We are not going to write the letters just yet," Ms. Colman told me. "First we are going to talk about the reasons we admire people."

Boo.

We talked, all right. We talked practically until recess. *Brrrnnng!* The bell rang.

Boo, boo, and double boo. I wanted to write my letter. I wanted to find out if I could get a costume like Irina's.

4

Winter Wonderland

During recess, snow started to fall. It was wet, icy snow. It turned to sleet. Soon the ground was very slick. Bobby Gianelli got an idea. He ran across the playground, then took a long slide. I tried it, too. It was just like skating!

"Look at me!" I yelled. "I am skating in the Olympics! I am going to win the gold medal!"

Ms. Colman called us inside then. It was too icy for us to play outside. Since it was still recess, Ms. Colman let us play games

16

at our desks. The sleet hit the windows. The cold, wet sound sent shivers up my back. Fun, wintry shivers.

When the bell rang, Ms. Colman sent us back to our desks. She wanted us to start on our letters. Finally! But just as I took out my paper, someone knocked at our door. It was the secretary from Mrs. Titus's office. Mrs. Titus is our principal. The secretary was holding a notice. She handed it to Ms. Colman.

"Well, class," Ms. Colman said. "This is some interesting news. Mrs. Titus has decided to close the school. She wants to send you home before the roads get too slippery. You may all put away your papers and put on your coats."

I looked at Hannie and Nancy. They looked at me. We would get another half day of vacation. Hurray! I did not shout this out loud, of course. I would never want to hurt Ms. Colman's feelings.

On the bus ride home, I looked out the window. The trees were covered with ice. It reminded me of a song, "Winter Wonderland." I started singing. Everyone joined in. Mr. Mundy, our bus driver, stopped the bus. He turned around and told us he could not see the road very well. He had to concentrate. He asked us to be more quiet. (He asked us nicely.) After that, I whispered the words to the song very quietly. The bus was slipping on the road. Mr. Mundy drove very slowly.

When I got home, I ran inside. But I did not take off my coat.

"Can I play outside?" I asked Mommy. "Please?"

Mommy looked doubtful. She peered out the window. Ice was now covering our yard. It was smooth and glassy.

"It looks a little slick out there," she said. "I do not know if it is safe."

"I will be careful," I promised. "I will not do anything dangerous. And you will be right here."

Mommy sighed. "You may play outside

for a few minutes," she said. "But you may not play in the tree house. That is too dangerous."

"I won't!" I cried.

Andrew stood behind Mommy. "Can I go too?" he asked.

"When you are bigger," said Mommy. "Now you can stay with me in the kitchen. You can help me mash the potatoes."

I was glad I was big enough to play outside in the stormy weather.

Outside, the ice was perfect. I slid around in my boots. I waved my arms gracefully like Irina Kozlova. I pretended I was wearing a wispy skating skirt. It had sequins on it. It was blue. No. Not blue. Purple.

Once I had seen Irina skate with a scepter in her hand. Maybe I should have my magic wand. The magic wand was up in the tree house, where Andrew had left it. I wanted to climb up and get it.

Hmm. Mommy had said not to play in the tree house, but I did not want to *play*

there. I only wanted to get the wand. Once I got it, I would come right back down. Then I would play in the yard.

I looked back at the window. Mommy was not watching. The steps to the tree house were covered with ice. I knew I would be safe if I held on tightly. I brushed the snow off my mittens and started to climb.

The Big Fall

The wand was in the tree house, just where I remembered. It was stuck in the ice. I chipped at the ice and pulled the wand free. I waved it high. "And now I will do a triple spin," I said, like Irina Kozlova. I started back down.

It was harder to climb down. I forgot that I would have to hold on to the wand. I clutched the wand in one hand and held on to the steps with the other. I looked down. Suddenly the tree house seemed awfully high. I took another step. Oops! My foot slipped. I tried to grab the step above me, but it was too late. I was already falling.

Bam! I landed face down on something hard. It was a tree stump sticking out of the snow. It had jabbed me right in my stomach. It really hurt. I tried to get up, but my stomach hurt even more when I moved. So I lay down in the snow again. The magic wand was lying beside me. Suddenly I did not feel very much like Irina Kozlova.

"Mommy!" I heard someone cry. It was Andrew. He was in the doorway. Oh, no! He had seen me fall. I struggled to get up. Now Mommy would know I had gone in the tree house.

Mommy came running outside. She was still in her apron.

"Karen!" she cried. "Are you all right? What happened?"

She knelt beside me.

"What hurts?" she asked.

"My stomach," I moaned. "Right here."

"Can you walk?"

"I think so."

"Come on." Mommy helped me. "I am going to call Dr. Dellenkamp. She will tell us what to do."

When we got in the house, Mommy told me to lie on the couch. I did not take off my coat or my boots or my hat. Mommy put a blanket over me to keep me even warmer. Then she called Dr. Dellenkamp.

"She says her stomach hurts," Mommy said. She looked at me from across the room. She looked worried. "Yes," she said. "She fell from quite a height."

When Mommy got off the phone, she told me we had to go to the hospital. Dr. Dellenkamp was going to meet us in the emergency room.

The emergency room? I had been there before. I had been there when I broke my wrist. "Do you think I broke something?" I asked.

"We do not know yet," said Mommy. "It is possible that you broke a rib."

Then Mommy called Mrs. Dawes next door. She explained what had happened.

"Can Andrew stay at your house?" she asked.

Mrs. Dawes said yes, of course.

Mommy bundled up Andrew. She put on her own coat, then called Seth at his workshop. She told him we were going to the hospital. She asked him to meet us there as soon as he could.

Mommy helped me to my feet. We got into the car. We watched to make sure Mrs. Dawes answered the door to let Andrew in. She stepped out onto the porch and put her arm around Andrew. They waved to us as we drove off.

Mommy drove slowly, just like the bus driver. The streets were still icy. It had started to sleet again. The sleet hit the windshield. The wipers scraped back and forth, back and forth. I remembered that Mommy had told me not to go up into the tree house. If I had listened, I wouldn't be hurt.

The pain in my stomach was getting worse. I settled back against the seat of the car and closed my eyes. It was a long, slow drive to the hospital.

The Hospital

When we reached the hospital, Seth was already waiting for us. The doctor in the emergency room took my pulse. He strapped something around my arm.

"I am going to take your blood pressure," he said. "This will not hurt at all."

The doctor was right. It did not hurt. Still, I squeezed Mommy's hand. I wanted to make sure she stayed close by.

"Hmm," the doctor said to Mommy and Seth. "We are going to need to take X rays."

Mommy nodded silently. They wheeled

me to the X-ray room and gave me a special X ray called a CAT scan.

The doctor looked serious. He did not say a word.

"We are going to have to admit Karen to the hospital," he told us at last.

Then they put me in a wheelchair. They wheeled me to *another* room. It had a bed. Seth helped me climb into it. Around the bed was a big white curtain.

Finally Dr. Dellenkamp arrived. She examined me too. She looked at my chart. She studied my X rays.

"So, Karen," she said. "Tell me what happened."

"Well," I said carefully. I did not want to look at Mommy. "I had to climb up into the tree house. *For just a minute.* Because the *magic wand* was up there. But on the way down, I fell on a tree stump."

"Where did it hit you?" asked Dr. Dellenkamp.

"Right here." I pointed to where it hurt.

29

Just then another doctor came into the room. He poked at my stomach. He talked softly to Dr. Dellenkamp and Mommy and Seth. I heard him say something about bleeding. Maybe this doctor did not understand.

"I am not bleeding," I told him.

"You are bleeding internally," Dr. Dellankamp answered. "That means you are bleeding *inside* your body."

The doctors and Seth and Mommy stepped outside the room to talk. I did not like the sound of this. Dr. Dellenkamp came back.

"It looks as if you have ruptured your spleen," she said.

I tried to remember what a spleen was. I thought of the science book that was in our classroom library. In it was a picture that showed the inside of the body. It showed the heart and the liver and the lungs and the intestines. I could not remember anything about the spleen.

"The spleen is on your left side," Dr. Dellenkamp explained. "Right where it hurts."

"What does rupture mean?" I asked.

"It means you might have torn the spleen and now it is bleeding."

This did not sound good. I thought of climbing down the icy tree-house steps. Now I *really* wished I had listened to Mommy.

"We are going to give you more blood," said Dr. Dellenkamp.

Uh-oh.

"And then we may have to do a little surgery."

Surgery!

"We will watch you this afternoon," said Dr. Dellenkamp. "We will see if you start to get better." She nodded to the other doctor. "But if your spleen is very damaged, Dr. Holter will take it out tonight. You will be okay after that. Your body can get better without your spleen."

I felt sick. I did not like the idea of hav-

ing surgery. I tried not to cry, but everything hurt. My eyes welled up. Mommy
squeezed my hand.

After the doctors left, a nurse came in.

"I am Brian," he said. "I am going to give
you more blood."

He hooked something to my arm.

"So," he said. "I heard that you were trying to ice skate."

"Like Irina Kozlova," I said.

"She is my favorite!" said Brian. "I watch
her every time she is on TV."

When he had finished, Mommy turned
down the lights in the room.

"I want you to close your eyes and get
some rest," she told me.

I closed my eyes. But I could not rest.

"Every time I close my eyes, I think of the
surgery," I told Mommy.

After awhile, the doctors came in to check
on me again. They told me I did not seem
to be getting any better. They decided they
would have to operate.

"The doctors will give you something to

make you sleepy," Mommy told me. "You will be asleep when they operate, and afterward you will probably sleep through the night. Tomorrow it will all be over."

It was nice to think of tomorrow. But it was still today.

"You are my brave girl," Mommy said. She patted my hand.

I looked around the cold, white hospital room. Somehow I did not feel as brave as Mommy thought I was. I did not feel very brave at all.

Sleepy, Sleepy Karen

The next thing I knew, I was waking up from a deep sleep. I opened my eyes. I was not sure where I was. A nurse was standing beside me. She told me my surgery was over.

"You are in the recovery room," she said.

I did not want to be in the recovery room. I wanted to be home. I wanted Mommy. I felt so groggy, and so very, very tired. I closed my eyes and fell asleep again.

When I woke up, I was back in the room with the bed and the curtain. A tube was in my arm. Goosie and Tickly were on the pillow next to my head. How had they gotten there?

Then I saw Mommy and Seth. They were sitting beside my bed. Mommy brushed the hair from my forehead.

"You did very well, Karen," she said. "Your surgery is over."

Mommy was smiling at me, but her eyes were wet. I think she had been crying.

"Mommy," I said. I started crying too. I did not know I was going to cry. It just happened. I tried to reach for Mommy, but my stomach hurt.

"Just lie still," she told me. "Your body needs to rest. It has been through a lot."

Mommy and Seth stayed with me all day. Daddy came to visit too. But no one else. I was too tired for visitors. I was still very sleepy from the surgery. But it was hard to sleep in the hospital. Nurses kept coming in and waking me up. They took my pulse. They took my temperature. Brian came in. He wanted to give me some shots. He reached for my arm. I pulled it away.

"Shots?" I asked. "What for?"

"Because we do not want you to get an infection," he said.

I let Brian take my arm. "Okay," I agreed. I did not want to get an infection. I already felt bad enough.

Mommy pulled her chair close to my bed.

"Would you like me to read to you?" she asked. She had brought a book with her. It was *The Cricket in Times Square* by George Selden.

That was a very good book, but I was too sleepy to pay attention. Still, I nodded yes. I liked the sound of Mommy's voice. When I was little, Mommy used to read to me all the time. Now I mostly read books by myself. But I did not feel so grown up in the hospital.

My eyes were heavy. I closed them. As Mommy read, I drifted back to sleep.

When I awoke again, the room was dark. Mommy was there, but nobody else. A nurse came in.

"I am Sylvia," she said. "I am going to take your temperature. I am glad to see that you have been resting."

"Where is Brian?" I asked.

"Brian is the day nurse," said Sylvia. "I will be your nurse during the night."

The hospital was a busy place. There were so many doctors, so many nurses. Too many for me to keep track of.

Mommy told me that visiting hours were almost over. When I went to sleep for the night, she would leave. She told me to call for Sylvia if I needed anything. Mommy kissed me on the forehead.

"Tomorrow I will come very early in the morning," she told me. "And you will have more visitors. Kristy will come and so will Nannie."

"Will Andrew come?" I asked. "Will Hannie and Nancy?"

"Only grown-ups," Mommy explained. "And older children like Kristy. Younger children cannot visit you in the hospital."

Boo and bullfrogs!

"But you will feel a little better tomorrow," Mommy said.

I put my head down on the pillow and hugged Goosie and Tickly. I hoped Mommy was right. I did not like feeling so sick.

A Visit to the Playroom

The next morning a nurse woke me up early. It was still dark outside. She took my temperature and checked the tube in my arm.

"What is this tube for?" I asked.

"It is called an IV," she explained. "It is a special tube for feeding you, since you cannot eat yet. In a day or two, you will start eating again. Then we will take it out."

A special tube! I felt very important.

"I hear you like Irina Kozlova," she said.

"How did you hear?"

"All the nurses know," she said. "You are famous around the hospital." She winked at me.

Just then Brian peeked in the room. He waved to me. I knew how she heard! Brian had told her.

Soon Mommy arrived.

"Hi, Mommy!" I cried. "I am famous! All the nurses know about me."

"Well, well," said Mommy. "It sounds as if you *do* feel better today."

That day, I had a lot of visitors. In the morning Daddy visited. Nannie came too. But she could not stay very long. She had to get home to watch Emily Michelle and Andrew. (Andrew was staying at the big house while I was at the hospital.)

When Daddy and Nannie had left, Brian came into the room.

"How is my favorite patient?" he asked.

"I have been busy," I said. "I have had a lot of visitors."

"That sounds like fun," he said. "And

41

now, how would you like to take a walk?"

"A walk? But where would I go?"

"There is a playroom at the end of the hall. You could go there."

"No thank you," I said. "I like it here in bed."

"Is it good for her to take a walk?" Mommy asked.

"Yes, it is," said Brian. "It will help her get stronger."

"But I am hooked up to the IV tube," I said.

Brian laughed. "The IV is on wheels," he explained. "You can wheel it along with you."

I pulled the bedsheet high around me. My tummy still hurt. I felt very weak. No one had told me I was going to have to take a walk.

"This is not fair," I said.

Mommy looked surprised. "You do not want to take a walk?" she asked.

I remembered what happened when I fell

42

out of the tree house. My stomach hurt more just thinking about it. "I might fall again," I said. "The floor might be slippery. Someone might bump into me." Suddenly, I was very afraid of accidents.

Mommy looked at Brian. She raised her eyebrows.

"Hey, champ," he said. "An old skating pro like yourself? You have nothing to be afraid of. Your mom and I will help."

Mommy and Brian started to help me out of bed.

"Wait!" I cried. "Not so fast!"

They let me go slowly. Mommy walked with me to the playroom. The toys there were old and broken. The paint was peeling off the walls.

"This is yucky," I said. "The playroom is stupid. I want to go back to bed."

Just then someone else came into the playroom. It was someone I knew! It was Christina. She is in second grade, just like me. She is in Mr. Berger's class.

"What are you doing here?" I asked.

Christina whispered something. I could hardly hear her.

"What?" I asked.

"I had my tonsils out," she whispered again. "My throat is too sore to talk."

I was glad to see Christina. We played very quietly. But I did not want to stay in the playroom long.

"It is important for me to rest," I explained to my friend. "Maybe I will see you later."

Mommy helped me walk back to my room. I walked slowly. Very slowly. I did not want to have another accident. I climbed back into bed.

"Do I have to walk any more today?" I asked.

Mommy looked at me for a moment. She fluffed my pillow.

"I think that is probably enough," she said.

"Mommy," I said. It was time for me to apologize. "I am very sorry I went into the tree house. You told me not to go. But I went anyway. That is why I had an accident. I will never do anything like that again. Accidents happen very fast. I did not know that."

"I am glad you will be more careful," said Mommy. "But I hope you will not always be so fearful."

Just then more visitors arrived. Sam and Charlie and Kristy and Elizabeth. Boy, was I glad to see them. Their arms were piled high with books and games.

"We brought you some things from home," said Kristy.

"Goody!" I cried.

I was happy to have things from home. Especially things I could do in *bed*.

Karen's Great Idea

The next morning I rang for Brian. That is something very fun about the hospital. You can ring for a nurse. All you have to do is press a button.

"Hello, Your Highness," Brian said when he saw me.

I was propped up on my pillows. I guess I looked like a queen.

"I would like an extra pillow, please," I said.

"Your wish is my command."

I giggled. I was getting very good at being in the hospital.

That day Seth came with Mommy to spend the morning with me. Mommy wanted me to walk to the playroom again.

"Do I have to?" I asked.

"You can show Seth how strong you are getting," she said.

I did not like walking in the hallway. Someone had just washed the floor. It was slippery. I was afraid I might fall. Nurses hurried past me with carts and trays.

"They are not being careful enough," I said to Mommy. "What if they bump into me?"

"Do not worry," she told me. "The nurses know how to be careful. That is part of their job."

When we reached the playroom, I saw Christina. She was sitting in a corner playing with a broken toy.

"I do not know why they call this a play-

room," she whispered. "There is not very much to *play* with here."

Then Christina told me she was leaving the hospital that day. Even though her throat still hurt, she was going home.

"I will come say good-bye to you before I go," she promised.

Later that day, I had a big surprise. Hannie and Nancy were on the lawn outside my window. Mrs. Dawes had brought them. They could not visit me inside the hospital, but they could come to my window!

"Halloooo up there!" they shouted up.

"Halloooo down there!" I called back.

"Pamela Harding skinned her knee!" they called.

Pamela Harding, my best enemy! Still, I was sorry to hear that she had skinned her knee. It just goes to show how easy it is to have an accident.

"She is lucky she didn't land on her spleen!" I shouted back.

Hannie and Nancy laughed. Then Mrs.

49

Dawes told them they had to go home.

"Good-bye, Hannie!" I called. "Good-bye, Nancy! I will see you soon!" Ooh. My tummy started to hurt. Maybe I should not have shouted so loudly.

Just then another visitor arrived. It was Ms. Colman.

"Hello, Karen," she said. She was laughing. "I see you still like to use your outdoor voice. Even in the hospital!"

Ms. Colman told me all about school. She told me about the projects our class was working on.

"Have you finished writing the letters?" I asked.

"We are finding all the addresses we need," she said. "It takes a bit of research. That is the last part of our project. Then we will mail the letters."

Hmm. I had not written my letter to Irina yet. I did not know if I wanted to now.

After Ms. Colman left, I turned on the TV. I flipped through the stations. On one station was a skating program. Irina Kozlova was on it! I watched as she jumped and turned. It looked more dangerous than I remembered. When she was through, everyone applauded. People threw flowers and stuffed toys on the ice for her. Irina skated around the rink, picking them up.

When Irina stepped off the ice, a reporter asked her a question.

"Irina," the reporter said, "what do you do with all the stuffed toys people give you?"

Irina smiled at the camera. "I am very grateful for all the presents," she said. Irina spoke with a Russian accent. "But I cannot use them all, of course. So I give them to a hospital. I hope the toys help the children in the hospital feel better."

A hospital. Irina gives the toys to a hospital. That gave me a good idea. I could not wait to tell Christina. When she came to my room to say good-bye, I said, "Christina, I have a *gigundoly wonderful* idea! When we go home, we can collect toys. Then we can donate the toys to the hospital."

I did not know exactly how we would do this, but I knew that I wanted to try.

Home Again

I did not have to stay in the hospital much longer. After a few more days, Dr. Dellenkamp said I could go home.

"But I do not want you to be exposed to any germs," she said. "You need to recuperate first."

"Recuperate?" I did not know what that meant. In the hospital, everyone used big words.

"It means you need to get well," she explained. "So I would like you to stay home from school for two weeks."

53

That sounded good to me.

When it was time to leave, Brian brought me a wheelchair.

"Good-bye!" I waved to all the nurses.

Mommy and Seth wheeled me to the car.

The car ride home was scary. The roads were slippery again. What if the car skidded on the ice? What if we had an accident?

When we got home, I went straight to my bed. Mommy helped me. Then she left me alone.

"Hmm," I said to myself. "What I need is a little bell. Then I could call Mommy and Seth like I called the nurses."

I remembered a bell I had won at a fair. It was in my drawer. I took it out and put it on the table next to my bed.

Tring-a-ling. I tried it out. No one came. *Tring-a-ling-a-ling!* I rang it again. Mommy came running. Perfect.

"What is the matter?" she asked.

"I would like a glass of water," I said.

Mommy looked a little angry. "If you want water, you can go into the bathroom."

54

"Dr. Dellenkamp said I have to stay in bed."

"No, she did not. She said you have to stay *at home*. It is good for you to move around."

I did not want to walk to the bathroom. What if I tripped on my toys or my shoes? What if the pipes burst? What if the hot water burned me?

"I might get in an accident," I said.

Mommy looked at me strangely.

"You can walk slowly," she told me. "As slowly as you want. If you are careful, you will not have an accident."

Boo and bullfrogs.

That day no one visited me until the afternoon. Hannie and Nancy were in school. In the meantime I needed a project. I decided to think about the toys for the hospital. I did not know how I would get them.

It is easy for Irina Kozlova, I thought. People throw the toys to her. All she has to do is skate around and pick them up.

I threw Goosie up into the air. Then I

pretended I was Irina, and scooped Goosie back up.

"Oh, what a beautiful stuffed toy," I said. I tried to talk with a Russian accent. "I think I will donate this beautiful toy to the sick children at the hospital."

Then I hugged Goosie. I was afraid Goosie would not know that I was pretending.

"Oh, Goosie, do not worry," I said. "I am not going to donate you to the hospital. I have to think of a way to get *other* toys."

Finally Hannie and Nancy arrived. They asked to see my stitches.

"I cannot show them to you," I said. "But I can show you my bandage."

Nancy stepped up to touch it.

"No!" I cried. I did not want Nancy touching my bandage. What if she touched too hard? What if she *fell* on me?

"It is *very* important that I do not have *any* more accidents," I said firmly.

Just then Andrew came to my doorway. He threw a ball into my room.

56

"Andrew!" I screamed. "You cannot throw things near me! I am *recuperating*! I have stitches!"

No one seemed to understand that I was still sick. No one was being as careful as I wanted them to be.

The Toy Drive

The next day I thought of a very good idea. If I wanted to get toys for the hospital, I could have a toy drive. I knew all about toy drives. I had worked on them before.

I could not wait for Hannie and Nancy to visit me that afternoon. I could not wait to tell them my idea.

"A toy drive," they said. "Like Kristy had for her softball team."

"Yes," I said. "And like the time we collected all our old toy guns. Only this time,

58

I will organize the toy drive. I can do everything from my bed. You can be my assistants."

"What do assistants do?" asked Hannie.

"Well, you can bring me the phone from the hall," I said. "That would be a good start."

Hannie brought me the phone. She pulled the long cord up to my bed.

"Now I will call Christina," I said. "She can organize a toy drive in her class too. That way we will have even *more* toys."

I did not have Christina's phone number by my bed.

"Nancy," I said. "Can you please get me the telephone book?"

Nancy ran to get the telephone book. This was working very well. I liked having assistants. It made it very easy to do things.

Then I called Christina. I told her about the toy drive. Christina liked the idea.

"I will make fliers for my class," I said. "Hannie and Nancy will bring them to school. They will give one to you. You can copy it and make some for your class, too."

"Should we ask our teachers if we can hand them out?" she said.

That was a good idea. "We will ask Ms. Colman and you can ask Mr. Berger," I said.

When I got off the phone, I asked Hannie to get me some paper.

"And some Magic Markers too!" I shouted after her.

Hannie stopped in the doorway. She came back into my room.

"You are being very bossy, Karen," she said.

Of course I was being bossy. It was my *job* to be bossy. I was the *boss*. I did not say this to Hannie, though.

I said, "But I cannot get out of bed."

"Still, you could be nicer," she told me.

"*Please*, would you get me some paper and Magic Markers?" I asked.

Hannie did.

Writing the flier for the toy drive was fun. We had to think of all the things we should say on the flier.

"Where should people bring the toys?" asked Nancy.

"They can bring them to my house," I said.

"Where will you put them?" asked Hannie.

"I will keep them in my room," I answered. "That way I can inspect them."

"Don't forget to write that the toys should be in good condition," said Nancy. "We do not want any broken toys."

After we thought of all our ideas, I wrote the flier. This is what I wrote:

DID YOU GET TOO MANY TOYS FOR CHRISTMAS OR HANUKKAH? ARE YOUR TOYS CLUTTERING UP YOUR HOUSE? GIVE THE TOYS YOU DO NOT WANT TO THE HOSPITAL! THE KIDS THERE NEED TOYS TOO! (PLEASE GIVE TOYS IN GOOD CONDITION ONLY.)

At the bottom, I wrote my address. Then I decorated the page with pictures of toys.

"There," I said. I smoothed the page.

"This is beautiful. Now we can make lots of copies."

"Do you think you should check with your mom first?" asked Hannie.

"I do not need to," I said. "I know she will say yes."

Hannie and Nancy looked at each other.

I wondered if Mommy would really say yes. I certainly hoped that she would.

Toys, Toys, and More Toys

"Karen!"

Mommy was calling me. She was at the front door. I had heard the doorbell ring.

"Yes, Mommy?" I called back.

"Can you come here, please?"

"I have to stay in bed!" I shouted.

"No, you do not. Come to the door now!"

Mommy did not understand that it was dangerous for me to get out of bed.

"I'm coming!" I called.

I walked very slowly.

64

At the door were Terri and Tammy, from my class. They were carrying three bags of toys.

"You told your friends to bring toys to our house?" asked Mommy. She was surprised.

"They are for a toy drive," I explained. "For the hospital."

"Where will you keep the toys?" asked Mommy.

"Oh, I have already decided that. I will keep them in my room."

Mommy sighed.

"Mommy," I said quickly, "you always tell me to help other people. And the children in the hospital *need* toys."

"Yes," she said, "but you need to remember to check with me first."

Terri and Tammy came inside. We opened their bags and looked through them. They had lots of good toys. They had brought two baby dolls, a toy telephone, and a bag full of dress-up clothes.

"The kids in the hospital will love these," I said.

"Did you talk to the hospital?" asked Mommy. "Did you find out if they will accept the toys?"

Oops. I had not.

"We could call Brian," I said. "He will tell us who to talk to."

"Take the toys to your room," said Mommy. "Then we will call."

Brian thought my idea was good. He told us to talk to a woman named Mrs. Silliman. She was the person in charge of the playroom. While we were on the phone, the doorbell rang again. More toys!

Over the next few days our doorbell kept ringing. Ricky Torres brought a big bag of books. Omar Harris brought some blocks and some puzzles. There was not enough space to store all the toys. Seth and Mommy stood in the doorway of my room. They looked at the bags and boxes.

"We are going to have to find some other place for the toys," said Mommy.

"How about the garage?" said Seth.

I thought of the garage. There were lots

of dangerous things there, things hanging on the walls. Sharp things. Metal things. What if they fell on me?

"I cannot bring the toys to the garage," I said. "Someone else will have to do it. It is too dangerous for me."

Mommy and Seth loked at each other.

"Karen," said Mommy. "The bags are probably too heavy for you to carry. Seth and I will help. But it is good for you to walk around. Soon you will be going back to school, you know."

"School?" I said. I had almost forgotten about school. School was going to be a problem.

"Sometimes kids run in the hallways," I said. "Sometimes they throw things on the playground. School is not a very safe place for me."

Mommy gave me a hug. "I think you will be fine once you get there," she said.

Karen's Letter

Soon it was Sunday. I would be going back to school the next day. I had a lot of work to do first. I had to inspect all the toys in the garage. There was only one problem. The toys were piled up, and I was afraid they would fall on me.

I borrowed a pad of paper from Mommy. Then I asked Andrew if he would help me. Andrew and I went to the garage. I stood in the doorway. I knew I could not get hurt there.

"You tell me what the toys are," I told

Andrew. "And I will write them down."

Andrew called out the names of the toys.

"Checkerboard!" he cried. "Toy piano!"

I made a list of the toys we had collected. I wanted to be able to tell everyone at school what a good job we had done.

"Karen!" Mommy called. "Andrew!"

Mommy was calling us to dinner. I walked carefully to the kitchen. Seth had made a big bowl of spaghetti.

"Yippee!" shouted Andrew. "Worms!"

Andrew was not the only one who was happy. Spaghetti was one of my favorite dinners.

"I am *sooooo* hungry!" I cried.

Mommy dished the spaghetti onto my plate. "So," she said, "tomorrow you will go back to school. Are you excited? You will see your friends again, and Ms. Colman."

I thought of all the accidents that could happen at school. They could happen very fast. It would be so much harder for me to be careful at school. I ate a bite of spaghetti. Suddenly I did not feel well. I pushed the

69

spaghetti around my plate. Mommy watched me.

"I thought you were hungry," she said.

"I was. But now my stomach hurts," I said. "Maybe I am getting sick."

I did not eat another bite. I did not feel like it.

After dinner Mommy told me to get in my pajamas. She let me lie in bed and watch television. Another skating program was on. I watched Irina Kozlova. This time I noticed that she had a bandage on her knee. The announcer said she had fallen in practice. He said that maybe she was going to have surgery.

As I watched, Irina fell again, right in front of everyone.

"Ow!" I cried out loud. It looked as if she had fallen very hard. But Irina did not lie on the ice. She got right up and continued her program. I did not think I could do that. Now I had a new reason to admire Irina. She was not afraid. I decided I would write her and tell her.

70

I got a piece of paper.

"Dear Irina," I wrote. "A few weeks ago I had a very bad accident. I had to go to the hospital. I even had to have surgery."

Then I told Irina all about the yucky old playroom. I told her about the toy drive I had planned.

"I admire you because you are very brave," I wrote. "I used to be brave too. But now sometimes I get scared.

"P.S.," I added. "I really love your costumes. I never see costumes like that in the stores. Do you buy them someplace special?"

The next morning Mommy came in my room. She woke me up to go to school. My stomach felt worse than ever.

"Maybe I have the flu," I said.

Mommy took my temperature.

"You do not have a fever," she said.

I held my stomach.

"Ooooh," I groaned.

Mommy felt my head. She looked worried.

"There is a flu going around," she said.

"Yes," I told her. "And it is not good for me to be exposed to so many germs."

Mommy looked out the window. It was windy and cold. She sighed.

"I do not want you to get sick," she said. "You can stay home for one more day. But tomorrow you will go back to school."

14

Back to School

When I opened my eyes on Tuesday morning, I had a stomachache again. Still, Mommy came in to wake me up. She turned the light on. She pulled up my shades and opened the door to my closet.

"What would you like to wear today?" she asked.

I knew Mommy meant business. I knew that she would not let me stay home from school even one more day. I tried to think of something I could wear to school.

"Two sweaters," I said.

"Two?" Mommy asked. "Why two? You will be so hot!"

"That way, if someone bumps into me, I will be padded," I explained.

I put on my red Christmas sweater. Then I put my blue taxi sweater on top. I looked in the mirror. I looked a little big.

Before I left, I ate a bowl of cereal. Quickly. Then I put on my coat.

"You do not need to leave yet," said Mommy. "The bus will not be here for another ten minutes. Wait inside awhile. You will be cold."

"I can't," I explained. "I am going to walk to the bus stop *very slowly*. It will take me a lot of time."

Mommy watched me from the window. I walked down our front walk. The sidewalk was still snowy. I took baby steps. I held my hands in front of me. That way, if I fell, I would land on my hands, not my stomach.

By the time I got to the bus stop, I was sweating. It was hard work being so careful. And this was only the beginning of the day.

"Hi, Karen!"

Nancy was running toward the bus stop. She was happy to see me. She started telling me about school.

"We just finished a very good writing project," she said. "We wrote poems about winter."

I nodded.

"We did worksheets about animals. We also learned a song about rivers."

All this talk was making me dizzy.

"Nancy," I said, "now that I am going back to school, I have to be very careful. I hope you do not mind, but I do not want to talk so much. I have to pay attention."

The bus drove up the street. Mr. Mundy smiled when I climbed up the steps.

"Karen," he said. "How are you? It is good to see you back."

"I am still recuperating," I told him. "Could you please drive carefully? It is not

75

good for me to be on a bumpy ride."

Mr. Mundy saluted me. "Aye, aye, captain!" he said.

Mr. Mundy thought I was kidding. I was not. I took a seat next to Nancy. I held tightly to the seat in front of me. Maybe the bus would skid or swerve.

Soon we were at school. I had forgotten how noisy the halls were. Kids were hurrying to their classrooms. Some were running in the hall. Where was the hallway patrol? They were supposed to make sure everyone walked *slowly*.

My classroom did not seem very safe either. Everyone was jumping around.

"Hi, Karen!" called Bobby Gianelli. He threw a book to Ricky.

"Hey!" I cried. "Watch what you are doing!"

Usually I stay in the back of the room, talking to Nancy and Hannie until the bell rang. But this time I walked straight to my desk and sat down. Finally Ms. Colman came into the room.

"Welcome back, Karen," she said. "We have all missed you. Would you like to take attendance this morning?"

"No, thank you," I said. "It is safer for me to sit right here."

After attendance, Ms. Colman told us to get out our pencils and rulers and scissors.

Pencils! Scissors! They were sharp and pointed. They could stab me and hurt me. I hoped everyone would be careful.

"Mrs. Titus has asked our class to make posters for the hallways," said Ms. Colman. "They will be public service announcements. That means they will have messages that are important for students to remember. Can you think of some messages you would like your schoolmates to keep in mind?"

I waved my hand wildly.

"Yes, Karen?" asked Ms. Colman.

"Safety!" I cried out. "It is a *lot* more important than people think."

Another Great Idea

Somehow I made it through the morning without getting hurt. Then the bell rang again. Oh, no. It was recess. Recess would be *very* difficult. As we lined up to go outside, I decided what I would do. I would stand at the side of the playground and lean against the building. Then the other kids would not run into me.

When we got outside, I saw Christina. She was all the way across the yard.

"Karen!" she called out. I guess her throat

felt better. She didn't have to whisper anymore.

"Hello!" I waved back. Christina ran to me.

"I have collected some toys for the hospital," she said. "Have you?"

"I have collected forty-two toys exactly," I said. I knew this because I had made a list. "All of our toys will look very good together in the playroom. Just think how happy they will make the kids in the hospital."

I paused a moment to think of the children playing with our toys. Christina thought too.

"But where will the hospital *put* the toys when we bring them?" she asked. "They only have one tiny shelf."

Hmmm. I had not thought about that. We had collected a lot of toys. They would not all fit on the small shelf. And they certainly could not be all over the floor.

"They would clutter up the playroom," said Christina.

80

"That would be dangerous," I said. "Someone could *trip* on them." Then I got an idea. "Hey," I cried. "When we bring the toys, we could fix up the playroom. I bet my stepfather could even build new shelves."

"We could paint the walls!" said Christina.

"And get new curtains!"

This was a gigundoly wonderful idea.

"We should talk to our teachers," said Christina. "This is a big job. We should get everyone to help."

After recess Christina and I found Mr. Berger and Ms. Colman. They were talking together in the hall.

"We have a *very* good idea for a project," I said. Then Christina and I told our teachers about the playroom.

"The toys we have collected are very nice," I said. "But there is a lot more work to be done. We need to fix up the playroom so it does not look so sad and run-down."

"That *is* a very good idea," said Ms. Colman. She smiled.

I knew Ms. Colman would like my idea.

"I think you should talk to the rest of the class," she said. "I will give you time to talk to them tomorrow."

Mr. Berger also liked the idea. He told Christina she could talk to her class the next day too. I hurried into the classroom and plopped down at my desk. I was so excited that I almost forgot to be careful.

That night at dinner, I told Mommy and Seth about the new part of my hospital project.

"We are going to fix up the playroom," I said. "We are going to paint and put up curtains and shelves." I looked at Seth. "Do you think you could help with the shelves?" I asked. "Are they very hard to build?"

Seth speared the peas on his plate. He took a bite and chewed.

"I could build some shelves," he agreed.

"And did you say you need curtains?"

82

asked Mommy. "Curtains are not hard to sew. I could make those."

"Really?"

This was turning out even better than I had imagined. I hoped that my classmates would want to help too.

Karen's Speech

That night, before I went to bed, I practiced the speech I would give to my class.

Seth poked his head in the door.

"How is the public speaking coming?" he asked.

"What is public speaking?" I asked.

"It is when you stand up in front of a group of people and give a speech," he said. "Some people are afraid to give speeches. Are you worried about tomorrow?"

"Oh, no!" I said. I looked in the mirror. I

spoke more loudly. I gestured with my arms. I had a feeling I was going to be very good at public speaking.

The next day in school, Ms. Colman called me to the front of the class.

"Karen wants to talk to you about something," she told my classmates.

I looked around at all the faces in the class. I cleared my throat to make sure everyone would pay attention. Then I gave my speech. This is what I said:

"Imagine if you were in the hospital. Imagine what it would be like to feel very, *very* sick and have nowhere to play."

Then I paused. I made my face sad so everyone would think seriously. Then I went on.

"Two weeks ago I was in the hospital. The hospital has a playroom, but it is not fixed up. Now we have new toys for the playroom. But the toys are not enough. The playroom is old and dirty. My mother said that she will make curtains. And my stepfather says that he will build shelves. But I

85

think we can *all* help. Do you have any ideas?"

The kids started to raise their hands.

Ms. Colman stepped up to the blackboard. She told everyone that Mr. Berger's class would be helping too. Then she wrote down the ideas people had. Some of the ideas were very good. Leslie Morris thought we should paint the walls. Natalie Springer said that we should also paint a *picture* on one of the walls.

"That is called a mural," said Ms. Colman. "A mural is a large painting on a wall. What would you like the picture to be?" she asked.

"Children running and playing!" cried Ricky.

I waved my hand. Ms. Colman called on me.

"That might make some children in the hospital feel bad," I said. "What if they can*not* run and play? Or what if they are *recuperating*? Maybe it is not *safe* for them to run and play."

Ms. Colman asked for other ideas.

"Guys playing basketball," said Bobby.

"Ballerinas dancing," said Pamela.

"Children playing with animals," said Hannie.

That seemed like a very good idea to me.

We took a vote. I voted for children and animals. Guess what. That was the idea that won.

"Goody!" I cried out.

Ms. Colman reminded me to wait my turn to speak.

After that we were very busy in class. We had a lot to do. First we had to figure out how we would get the paint we would need.

Then Ms. Colman told us that she would call the hospital. She would talk to Mrs. Silliman and plan a good day for us to come and work.

Suddenly I thought of something. I raised my hand. "I cannot carry big cans of paint," I told Ms. Colman. "They are too heavy for me. They might bang against my stomach."

"That is okay," said Ms. Colman. "Everyone will do what they can."

Then she told us to take out our paper and pencils. We each made a sketch of what we thought the mural should look like. Everyone was busy. I felt very proud. All of this work was because of me.

Animals, Animals Everywhere

That afternoon, after school, I called Christina. I told her what the kids in my class had decided to do. Christina told me what had happened in her class.

"Someone is going to donate a rug," she said.

"A rug!" I said. "What a good idea! That will make the playroom *very* warm and cozy."

"The rug has pictures of animals on it," said Christina.

90

Animals! This was perfect. "Our mural is going to have animals in it too."

When I hung up, I ran to Mommy.

"Mommy," I said. "I have an idea for the curtains. I think they should have animals on them. Then *everything* in the playroom would have animals."

"That would be nice," said Mommy. "I am going to the store this weekend. You can help me pick out the material."

Just then Seth came home.

"Well," he said, "I have good news for you, Karen. I have made the measurements for the shelves."

"Excellent!" I cried.

I had a lot of things to tell my class when I went back to school.

The next day I was not the only one with good news to report. Ms. Colman told us that she had talked to Mrs. Silliman at the hospital.

"We will go to fix up the playroom two weeks from now," she said. "We will go on a Friday morning and stay all day."

I raised my hand. I told my class about the animal theme. I told them that Seth was working on the shelves.

"Maybe we could paint animal pictures on the shelves, too," Addie suggested.

Every day we were thinking of more things to do.

Later in the week, Ms. Colman brought in an article she had found in a magazine. It was about people who are sick. The article said that animals often make people feel better. When people play with animals, it helps them get well.

"Maybe our animal pictures will help," she said. "It will remind people of the pets they have at home."

See why Ms. Colman is such a good teacher?

On Saturday, Mommy and I went shopping. We headed straight for the fabric store. At first I did not see any fabric with animals on it. I saw bright red fabric. I saw plaid fabric. I saw fabric with checks and fabric with gold threads running through it.

"Oooh," I said. "This is very beautiful. It would make a wonderful costume for Irina Kozlova. But it is not good for our curtains."

Mommy asked the saleswoman for help.

"Animals," she said. She stopped to think. "I have one bolt of fabric with animals on it. It is in the back. I will bring it out for you to see."

I crossed my fingers and held my breath. The saleswoman came back out with a bright bolt of fabric. It was covered with pictures of monkeys and giraffes.

I grinned at Mommy.

Mommy laughed. "I think that means you like it," she said.

"I do!" I cried. "I like it very much."

The Big Day

Finally the big day arrived. My classmates and I had worked very hard. We were ready to fix up the playroom. That morning, I woke up bright and early. I ran to the window and looked outside. Goody! It was not snowing. We would have no trouble getting to the hospital.

Seth was awake too. I found him in the garage. He was loading things into his van. He was stacking up the toys and the long, flat boxes with Mommy's curtains in them. I waved to him from the door.

"Good morning, Karen," he said to me. "Better get dressed. We have a big day ahead of us."

Oops! I was still in my pajamas.

In my room I thought carefully about what I would wear. I should wear old clothes. We would be cleaning and painting. I put on an old pair of jeans. Then I found a long, sloppy shirt that used to be Kristy's. She had given it to me to play in. I put on my oldest shoes. I *certainly* did not want to get paint on any of my good shoes.

When I went downstairs to breakfast, Seth came inside to say good-bye.

"I am going to my workshop to pick up the shelves," he said. "I will meet you at the hospital."

I put on my coat and kissed Mommy.

"Have fun!" she said as she waved good-bye.

Then I headed for the bus. The sidewalk was still slippery. By now, though, I was very good at taking baby steps. I walked to the bus inch by inch.

At school everyone looked funny. No one was wearing school clothes. Everyone was in old clothes. I spun around to show Hannie my big shirt. It puffed out like a sail. As soon as everyone arrived, we gathered up our supplies. Then Ms. Colman told us to sit down. She told us how we should behave at the hospital.

"We should be very quiet in the halls," she said. "People there do not feel well. We need to be careful not to disturb them. We should not run and we should not shout."

I raised my hand to speak.

"Also," I said, "we cannot visit the children who are sick."

"That is a good point," said Ms. Colman. She smiled at me.

I knew all about the hospital. I knew all the rules.

Then we lined up and got on the bus. Mr. Berger's class got on too.

"We should sing songs," I said. "Animal songs."

It was not easy to think of animal songs. But we did. We sang "How Much Is That Doggy in the Window?" We sang "Two Little Ducks." Then we sang "Teddy Bears' Picnic." Before we knew it, we had arrived at the hospital. We got off the bus and walked to the front desk.

Inside the hospital, I felt a little scared. The smell of the building reminded me of being sick. I put my hand over my tummy to protect it. Maybe it was not such a good idea for me to be fixing up the playroom.

Mrs. Silliman was waiting at the front desk to meet us. She introduced herself.

"It is very nice of you to help us fix up the playroom," she said. "Which one of you is Karen Brewer?"

I shot up my hand.

"Karen," she said, "you can help me lead your schoolmates to the children's floor."

When we reached the playroom, Seth was already there. His shelves were stacked on their sides. His tool kit was open. I could see hammers and saws and drills and nails.

Everyone hurried into the room to get busy. I stayed in the doorway. Suddenly this did not feel like a very safe place for me to be.

Welcome Home!

Seth saw me standing in the doorway. He waved to me. Just then, Mr. Berger clapped his hands. He told everyone to sit on the floor. Then Mr. Berger and Ms. Colman told us all the jobs that needed to get done. They asked for volunteers.

One by one, my friends raised their hands and volunteered for jobs. Nancy wanted to sketch our animal picture onto the sides of the shelves. Christina wanted to hang mobiles by the window. (Her class had made mobiles from cellophane. When the sun shone through them, the light changed color!) Hannie wanted to paint the big, plain wall. She got a paint roller. I was the last one in the circle. I did not volunteer for anything.

"Karen," asked Ms. Colman, "what would you like to do?"

I had to think of a safe idea.

"I think I will help Nancy," I decided. "I am very good at drawing."

The day went by fast. At noon Ms. Silliman brought lunch for us. We ate chicken soup and green Jell-O.

After I finished sketching, I helped Seth screw the shelves into the wall. Then I helped paint them.

Brian the nurse poked his head in the door.

"Hey, Karen!" he called to me. "Hello!"

"Hello!" I cried back. I waved my paintbrush at him. Uh-oh! Paint splattered on the floor and in Nancy's hair. I grabbed a paper towel and cleaned it up quickly.

Brian laughed.

"I see you are as busy as ever," he said.

At the end of the day, the room looked beautiful. It was bright and clean and cheerful. The sun streamed through Mommy's curtains. Pictures of animals were everywhere.

"Congratulations!" I shouted to my friends. "We have done a *very* good job!"

Ms. Colman tapped me on the shoulder. "Indoor voice," she reminded me.

Then it was time to help Seth carry in the boxes of toys. They were still in the van. We put on our coats. We paraded out to the parking lot. Seth handed each of us a box or a bag. We walked in a long line back to the playroom.

"We look like a train," I said.

Hannie giggled.

We could not put the toys on the shelves, though. The shelves were still wet with paint. Ms. Silliman promised us that she would arrange the toys later. Then she gave a speech.

"I want to thank you all very much for

101

coming," she said. "The playroom looks beautiful. You did a wonderful job."

Afterward Ms. Colman added a special thanks. It was to Christina and me.

"I am sure we all want to thank Karen and Christina," she said. "They suggested this project. If they had not, the playroom would still be old and sad looking."

I felt very proud. I thought of all the children who would use the room. Maybe it would help them get better. I smiled at Christina. She smiled back at me.

The Best Surprise

Finally it was time to go home. Everyone got back on the bus. Everyone except Nancy and me, that is. Ms. Colman said we could go home with Seth. Now that the shelves and the toys were out of the van, there was plenty of room for us.

All the way home, I talked about the playroom.

"The best part is the murals," I said. "No, wait! The best part is the shelves! No, I mean the curtains! Hmmm." I could not decide. "The mobiles look cool too."

"I think the rug looks nice," said Nancy. That was true too.

Seth was driving carefully. He was watching the road. I remembered I had better thank him.

"You and Mommy did *so* much work," I said. "Thank you very much. We were all very glad you could make the shelves." (That gave me another idea. Maybe I would ask my class to write a special thank-you note to Seth and Mommy. I was sure Ms. Colman would think that was a good idea.)

Seth pulled into our driveway. I stepped out of the van. The driveway was icy and slippery. Sleet was falling on my glasses. It made everything look smeary.

"How long has it been sleeting?" I asked.

"All the way home," said Seth.

It had been sleeting and I had not even noticed. And I had not worried all day at the hospital, either. I had been so busy, I did not have time to worry.

I sighed a big, heavy sigh. I did not

want to worry anymore. It was hard work to worry all the time.

"Can Nancy stay and play awhile?" I asked Seth.

"Sure," he agreed.

Nancy and I ran inside to tell Mommy about the day. On the front walk, I slid on the ice. On purpose!

"Look, Nancy!" I cried. "I am skating again!"

Mommy was in the living room, reading a book.

"Mommy! Mommy!" I cried. "The playroom looks beautiful! Your curtains look perfect! There are mobiles at the windows too! And Brian the nurse came to say hello! I spilled a little bit of paint, but I wiped it right up so it did not matter. And — "

"Wait a minute, wait a minute." Mommy laughed. "Let's get your coat off. Would you girls like some warm cider?"

"Yes," we cried.

"Oh," said Mommy. "I almost forgot. A

package arrived for you, Karen. It came this afternoon."

A package? For me? I did not know who it could be from. Christmas was over. And my birthday was not for a long time.

"The package is in the front hall," said Mommy.

Nancy and I ran to see what it was.

I did not see a return address on the package. I tore open the box. Inside was a present. On top was a letter. It was from Irina Kozlova!

"Dear Karen," she wrote.

"I am sorry to hear that you had an accident. Soon I will go into the hospital for surgery too. The doctors say I have to have an operation on my knee. You told me you think I am brave, but I think *you* are brave. When I go into the hospital, I will think of you. It sounds as if you have done very good work collecting toys for the hospital. I am sending you a stuffed animal for your toy drive. I hope it is not too late. Thank

you for writing to me. Irina Kozlova.

"P.S. I do not get my costumes at a store. A designer makes them for me. She sews on all the sequins by hand. Good luck to you!"

(Hmm, I thought. *Mommy* sews. Maybe sometime she could sew a costume for *me*!)

Nancy and I dug down into the box. Inside was a big stuffed monkey.

"Wow! That is cool!" said Nancy.

"It will go perfectly with the curtains!" I cried.

Mommy called us into the kitchen. Now I had even *more* to tell her. Our cider was warm and delicious. It had been a *very* good day.

About the Author

ANN M. MARTIN lives in New York City and loves animals, especially cats. She has two cats of her own, Gussie and Woody.

Other books by Ann M. Martin that you might enjoy are *Stage Fright*; *Me and Katie (the Pest)*; and the books in *The Baby-sitters Club* series.

Ann likes ice cream and *I Love Lucy*. And she has her own little sister, whose name is Jane.

Little Sister

Don't miss #82

KAREN'S SECRET VALENTINE

"Tomorrow is our Valentine's Day party," announced Ms. Colman. "We will have special Valentine's Day refreshments. And we will find out who our Secret Valentines are."

I wiggled in my seat. I could not wait to find out who my Secret Valentine was. That morning I found a heart-shaped sugar cookie in my desk.

What would Pamela think when she found out I had been her Secret Valentine? I had been a good Secret Valentine. But would she blame me for the mean things she had gotten? Someone was still sending Pamela mean notes almost every day. And once that week she had found a dried-up earthworm on her desk. It had been very gross. But it had not been me.

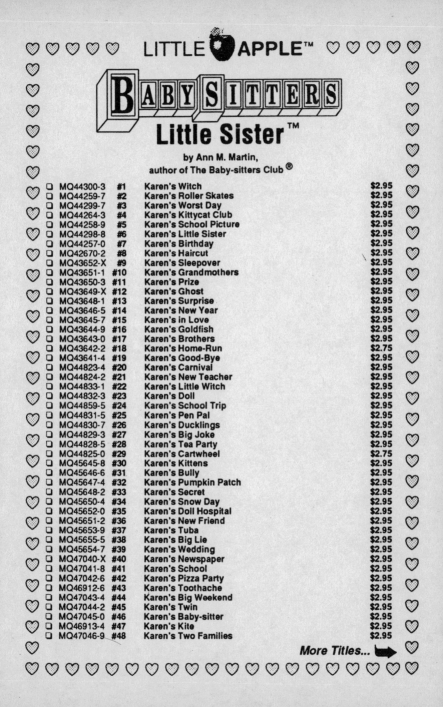

LITTLE APPLE™

BABY SITTERS
Little Sister™

by Ann M. Martin,
author of The Baby-sitters Club ®

More Titles... ➡

The Baby-sitters Little Sister titles continued...

☐	MQ47047-7	#49	Karen's Stepmother	$2.95
☐	MQ47048-5	#50	Karen's Lucky Penny	$2.95
☐	MQ48229-7	#51	Karen's Big Top	$2.95
☐	MQ48299-8	#52	Karen's Mermaid	$2.95
☐	MQ48300-5	#53	Karen's School Bus	$2.95
☐	MQ48301-3	#54	Karen's Candy	$2.95
☐	MQ48230-0	#55	Karen's Magician	$2.95
☐	MQ48302-1	#56	Karen's Ice Skates	$2.95
☐	MQ48303-X	#57	Karen's School Mystery	$2.95
☐	MQ48304-8	#58	Karen's Ski Trip	$2.95
☐	MQ48231-9	#59	Karen's Leprechaun	$2.95
☐	MQ48305-6	#60	Karen's Pony	$2.95
☐	MQ48306-4	#61	Karen's Tattletale	$2.95
☐	MQ48307-2	#62	Karen's New Bike	$2.95
☐	MQ25996-2	#63	Karen's Movie	$2.95
☐	MQ25997-0	#64	Karen's Lemonade Stand	$2.95
☐	MQ25998-9	#65	Karen's Toys	$2.95
☐	MQ26279-3	#66	Karen's Monsters	$2.95
☐	MQ26024-3	#67	Karen's Turkey Day	$2.95
☐	MQ26025-1	#68	Karen's Angel	$2.95
☐	MQ26193-2	#69	Karen's Big Sister	$2.95
☐	MQ26280-7	#70	Karen's Grandad	$2.95
☐	MQ26194-0	#71	Karen's Island Adventure	$2.95
☐	MQ26195-9	#72	Karen's New Puppy	$2.95
☐	MQ26301-3	#73	Karen's Dinosaur	$2.95
☐	MQ26214-9	#74	Karen's Softball Mystery	$2.95
☐	MQ69183-X	#75	Karen's County Fair	$2.95
☐	MQ69184-8	#76	Karen's Magic Garden	$2.95
☐	MQ69185-6	#77	Karen's School Surprise	$2.99
☐	MQ69186-4	#78	Karen's Half Birthday	$2.99
☐	MQ69187-2	#79	Karen's Big Fight	$2.99
☐	MQ69188-0	#80	Karen's Christmas Tree	$2.99
☐	MQ55407-7		BSLS Jump Rope Rhymes	$5.99
☐	MQ73914-X		BSLS Playground Games	$5.99
☐	MQ89735-7		BSLS Photo Scrapbook Book and Camera Package	$9.99
☐	MQ47677-7		BSLS School Scrapbook	$2.95
☐	MQ43647-3		Karen's Wish Super Special #1	$3.25
☐	MQ44834-X		Karen's Plane Trip Super Special #2	$3.25
☐	MQ44827-7		Karen's Mystery Super Special #3	$3.25
☐	MQ45644-X		Karen, Hannie, and Nancy	
			The Three Musketeers Super Special #4	$2.95
☐	MQ45649-0		Karen's Baby Super Special #5	$3.50
☐	MQ46911-8		Karen's Campout Super Special #6	$3.25

Available wherever you buy books, or use this order form.

Scholastic Inc., P.O. Box 7502, 2931 E. McCarty Street, Jefferson City, MO 65102

Please send me the books I have checked above. I am enclosing $ _____
(please add $2.00 to cover shipping and handling). Send check or money order – no cash or C.O.Ds please.

Name _____ Birthdate _____

Address _____

City _____ State/Zip _____

Please allow four to six weeks for delivery. Offer good in U.S.A. only. Sorry, mail orders are not available to residents to Canada. Prices subject to change.

BLS5962

The Adventures of
MARY-KATE & ASHLEY™

Read our Books!

Mary-Kate and Ashley Olsen — the stars of television, movies, videos, and music — are now the stars of their very own books! Based on their best-selling videos, this super series features Mary-Kate & Ashley as the Trenchcoat Twins™ — a pair of detectives who "Will Solve Any Crime By Dinner Time.™" Catch up with the super-duper snoopers in these fun-filled books!

Look for these at a bookstore near you!

SCHOLASTIC | DUALSTAR PUBLICATIONS PARACHUTE PRESS, INC.